Smart Girls

Books by the same author

Idle Jack
Smart Girls Forever
Why is the Cow on the Roof?

Robert Leeson
Smart Girls

illustrated by
Axel Scheffler

**WALKER
BOOKS**

For Christine

This is a work of fiction. Names, characters, places and incidents
are either the product of the author's imagination or, if real, used
fictitiously. All statements, activities, stunts, descriptions, information
and material of any other kind contained herein are included for
entertainment purposes only and should not be relied on for
accuracy or replicated as they may result in injury.

First published 1993 by Walker Books Ltd
87 Vauxhall Walk, London SE11 5HJ

This edition published 2017

2 4 6 8 10 9 7 5 3 1

Text © 1993 Robert Leeson
Illustrations © 1993, 2017 Axel Scheffler

ISBN 978-1-4063-8054-5

www.walker.co.uk

MIX
Paper from
responsible sources
FSC® C020471

Contents

SMART GIRLS – that's what they are:

Mary, Fionna, Kari, Marusya and Zaina.

Smart Girls are afraid of nothing and no one, alive or dead. Smart Girls have no time for big mouths or big heads, but Smart Girls are kind to fools, because fools have their uses.

Smart Girls don't always want to marry, but if they do, no one shall dare harm their husbands.

When Smart Girls are silent while others talk, it's because they are working out the answers to riddles no one else can answer.

Smart Girls never forget who has helped them, and they return the favour in good measure.

Smart Girls are everywhere and everywhen. These old-new tales come from England, Ireland, Norway, the Ukraine and Egypt. Sometimes they have travelled round the world.

And now they're told again for today's Smart Girls.

Mary

Mary

Mary was a maid. She worked in a house deep in a dark wood, down a long winding road, two miles beyond the village. To reach it you had to pass the ruined church where gravestones glinted white in the moonlight – if the moon shone. Then over the narrow bridge where the deep stream murmured in the gloom and up the twisting lane where hanging branches cast shifting shadows.

When the master's friends came for a drink on winter evenings, to sing and tell stories of ghosts and goblins, once they'd set foot inside the door and got their places by the blazing fire, they were in no hurry to venture out again.

And why should they be? Mary would cook their supper and fetch their beer, then, when they were tired, would make up their beds, light the candle and lead them up the stairs to sleep. In the morning they could go home in safety.

But one night, one dark, blustery, rainy night, they talked and sang and drank so well, the beer ran out. The barrel was dry and all the guests were down in the mouth.

"Someone'll have to go down the old lane to the village and get some more," thought one man. The others nodded and looked at one another. It was a splendid idea, but no one wanted to go.

Then the master himself spoke up. "Our Mary'll go," he said.

The others laughed. "What, a bit girl go down the old lane, over the bridge, past the churchyard and back, when there ain't even no moon? Never. If we daren't, how can she?"

The master answered, "Mary's a dauntless maid, she is. She fears nothing and no one, alive or dead."

"I don't believe you," said one of the drinkers.

"Suit yourself," said the master. He put money on the table. "Here's five pounds says she will."

"Done," said the other, digging in his pocket. "Here's five pounds says she won't."

But, she did. She picked up the big jug, threw on her shawl and off she strode. And an hour later back she came with the beer, and not a drop spilt. The master won his bet and put his five pounds in his pocket.

Mary watched the money change hands and said nothing. But she thought a bit.

Next day, when the guests left for home, the one who'd lost the bet asked the master, "You reckon there's nothing your Mary daren't do?"

"That's it," said he.

"Right. Here's fifty pounds says I can think of something she daren't do."

"Done, give us your money now, for it's as good as spent."

"You reckon?" said the guest.

And next week, he came back and told the master. "I say Mary daren't go down to the old church at midnight..."

"Course she dare."

"That's not all. She's to go right into the ruined crypt under the ground, look in that pile of bones there and bring a skull back, to prove it."

The master stared. But he had to call Mary and ask her. When Mary said "Why not?" the guest laughed to himself because he was certain of his fifty pounds. He'd bribed a village lad to hide in the crypt and scare the girl out of her wits.

At dead of night Mary set out down the windy lane, whistling to herself and swinging her lantern. When she got to the crypt, the rusty key was there in the ancient studded door. She went straight in, for the door stood half open.

Inside, it was as dark as pitch and smelt of death. In the blackness there were strange stirrings and rustlings. But Mary took not a bit of notice. She set down the lantern by the great pile of bones – arm bones, leg bones, finger bones, toe bones and skulls with their empty eyes.

Just as she had a nice one in her hands, the lad who was hiding let out a high-pitched moaning sound.

"Ooooooooh, Mary, girl, Mary girl!"

"What is it, you daft old thing?" she asked.

"Ooooooooh, Mary, don't 'ee take that skull, that be my mother's head..."

"All right," said Mary, "I'm not one to upset anybody. I'll take this'n."

"Ooooooooh, Mary," whimpered the lad, getting into his stride, "don't 'ee touch that'n, that be my father's."

"All the same to me," answered the girl. "Mother, father, grandad, they're all bones." And she took another.

The lad began to get a mite desperate now. He pitched his voice up till it almost broke.

"Ooooooooh, Mary," he began, but she'd had enough.

"I haven't all night to pick and choose. I'll have this one and that's that." So she took the skull, tucked it under her arm, picked up her lantern and marched out of the crypt. As she left, she called back, "'Tis powerful draughty in here. I'll close the old door for you."

She turned the key in the lock and set off for her master's house. As she came out of the dark into the warm sitting-room with the blazing fire, and planted the skull in the middle of the table, the guests were goggle-eyed.

None more than the man who'd bet, and lost, his fifty pounds. "Didn't you hear any ghost when you were down in the dead house?" he asked.

"Oh ah," she replied, "some stupid old thing was going on about all they skulls belonging to his mum and his dad. But I took no notice and just to be sure he didn't frighten anyone else, I locked him in."

They all began to laugh and the fifty pounds were paid over to the master. Mary watched the money disappear into his pocket.

She said nothing, but she thought a lot.

As to the man who'd lost the bet, he sneaked off to the church to let out the lad, who was half out of his mind with terror. So the man had to give him another five pounds to keep his mouth shut. It was an expensive evening.

Mary's fame spread far and wide till it reached the owner of the big Hall in the village. He thought to himself, a girl who's afraid of nothing – bright, capable and wins money for her master – that's the servant I need.

He had troubles. The Hall was haunted by his mother's ghost. When his mother was alive, he'd been afraid of her. Now she was dead, he was terrified.

But that wasn't all. No one would visit him because no sooner were they all seated at table in the dining-room than the old lady would slip in and start moving the dishes and the cutlery about, till the guests quite lost their appetite.

Worse still, not a single servant would stay in the place. The gentleman owner was in a state.

So he asked Mary to come and keep house for him. And Mary agreed because she thought to herself, he can't be meaner than my old master. She took the job.

Waiting at table, she watched the old ghost shifting things about. But she said nothing. She simply laid an extra place, with knife and fork and said, "There you are, whoever you are. Sit down and stop bothering other folk."

As the meal went on and the dishes came up from the kitchen, she offered each one to the ghost, saying, "Would you like the salt?" or "Would you care for the pepper?"

This so pleased the old ghost lady that everyone was able to eat their meal in peace. Now that pleased the owner and life went on.

But one day when Mary was alone in the house, cleaning the fireplace, she felt a little chill breeze on the back of her neck.

"Ah, there you are," she said cheerfully.

"What do you want this time?"

The ghost was taken aback. So surprised was she that for the first time she spoke.

"Aren't you afraid of me, Mary, like everyone else?"

"Not I," said Mary. "For I'm alive and you're dead."

That flummoxed the ghost so that for a minute she almost forgot what she'd come for. Then she told Mary, "Follow me, to the cellar."

Mary followed her down the gloomy stone steps. The ghost lit the way ahead with an eerie radiance. That didn't bother Mary, because it saved on candles.

In the corner of the cellar the old ghost pointed to the wall.

"See that brick. Pull'n out."

Mary did and out tumbled that brick, followed by two or three more. Behind lay a deep hole in the wall and at the bottom lay something soft and heavy. Mary reached in and felt around with her hand. There were two canvas sacks, one large, and one small. She heaved them out, and as she did they clinked and rattled.

"That's gold, Mary," whispered the ghost. "Now it's found, I can rest in peace. One bag is for your master and one is for you. You ask him. He'll know which is which."

"I'll wager he will," thought Mary.

With this, the ghost vanished. Not another word did she say, nor was she ever seen again, though some say that Mary crossed a pair of knives and forks at table just in case.

Imagine how pleased the owner of the house was when he came home.

"Why, Mary, how capital. That's a big one for me and a little one for you, for being a good girl."

"Ah," said Mary, "a good girl I may be but I'm not that much worse than you. If it hadn't been for me, you wouldn't have had either bag."

And he had to agree that was true. He couldn't think of what to do or say.

But Mary winked at him. "There's one way we can both fairly get our hands on both bags," she said. And the owner, who was not a fool, smiled and nodded to her.

"I reckon you are right, Mary."

So, they got married. And if they had any trouble after that, it wasn't with ghosts.

Fionna

Fionna

Fionna sat at her cottage door in the morning sunshine. While her hands and feet were busy with the spinning-wheel, her eyes were free to look down the road. On market days there were always people going to and fro and so it was today.

The first to come by were so strange that Fionna almost fell from her stool with laughter. Along came a sheep, wandering from side to side on the road, urged on by a tall young man with red hair.

From the dust on his jacket and the trowel in his belt she guessed he was a stonemason. But what was he doing taking a sheep to market? As the lad came closer, Fionna, being a kind girl, set her face straight and called out, "Hello and good morning to you."

He turned as red as a beetroot, put down

his head and hurried by without a word. The sheep only said "Ma-aaaaaaaa" and went by as well. Soon both had gone from sight.

But not from Fionna's mind. As the day passed, her spinning-wheel whirled and the sun turned from east to west, she thought of the boy with the sheep. She thought of his broad shoulders, his handsome open face and the way he'd blushed. A good lad, but a bit of a fool, perhaps. She sat and spun and waited. For she knew he would come again on the homeward road.

And he did, as the sun was setting. First came the sheep, though, footsore and complaining, then the lad, in no better shape. This time, Fionna called out, "Hello and good evening to you!"

Once again he turned red, red as the sun, and tried to sneak past, but Fionna stopped her wheel and stood up.

"Will you sit down and have a glass of milk?"

He slowed down and mumbled something.

So Fionna spoke a little more sharply.

"Can you not at least let the poor ewe have a drink from the beck?"

This did the trick. The lad turned from the road on to the grass by the cottage while the sheep, who caught the meaning, scrambled down to the stream and drank thirstily.

"What's your name, sir?" smiled Fionna.

"Ian." The lad looked at her, then away.

"Well, Ian, I am Fionna and you can see what I do for my bread. And I can see what you do for yours. But tell me, why is a young stonemason walking to and fro with a sheep?"

Ian hung his head, then burst out, "It's my father!"

"Your father? And who might he be?"

The boy looked proudly at her. "My father is the Gobán Saor, the Master Builder."

"Aha, the Master Builder," said Fionna. "I've heard of him and who has not? The castles he builds are the talk of the land. And what is his son doing trotting like a lamb behind its mother?"

Now the lad blushed into the neck of his shirt, drank his milk down and mumbled, "He set me a test."

"What sort of a test?"

"I must take the sheep to market, get ten pounds for it and bring it back home as well."

Fionna laughed. "And did you?"

The boy was angry now.

"You can see with your own eyes I didn't. No one would buy on those terms."

"So, you're off home to tell your da that you've failed?"

"I am."

Fionna laughed again.

"Well, Ian, you're a bit of a fool."

He frowned.

His eyes flashed with temper. Then he said, "That's just about it. My dad's a wise man, and I'm a fool. The shame of it!"

"Listen to me, Ian. I'll give you ten pounds."

His mouth fell open.

"You will?"

"Not for your lovely blue eyes, though. Bring the sheep up to the door."

While Ian did that, Fionna went inside the cottage and came out with shears.

"That's a fine fleece on the ewe," she remarked and – *snip, snip, snip* – she had the wool off the sheep's back.

"Now, Ian. That's ten pounds for the part of the sheep that I shall keep, while you take home the rest."

Ian knocked his head with his fist.

"What a fool I am."

"So you are, Ian. But no harm's done. Off you go. Give my greetings to your father and ask him when he'll have time to build me a castle."

Ian stared at her.

"You're pulling my leg."

"So I am. Does it hurt?"

Ian walked off down the road, with the sheep in front of him and ten pounds in his pocket and his heart light inside him. As he went, he heard the girl call.

"Come back again when your father sets you another impossible task. Maybe I'll have the answer."

Grinning, he turned and waved and then vanished into the dusk.

But one day, in early spring, as Fionna sat by the cottage door, she saw Ian again. He was marching along the road. Yes, marching. He had on a new blue jacket with a silver buckle at the belt and a hat with a green feather. He was alone, too.

Fionna called, "Hello and good morning to you! And where is the sheep?"

Ian drew closer, his sunburnt face was a little pink. He was smiling, a little foolishly.

"The sheep is at home, growing wool, and I have come on my own."

"Oh, and what test has the Master Builder set for his son today?"

Ian sat down while Fionna brought him a cup of milk. He drank it and said nothing.

"Well," she said. "Is the test too hard to even ask me?"

He took a deep breath, swallowed, looked at Fionna, then looked away. His face was crimson red again. Now Fionna laughed till the tears came.

"No need for you to say. I know the question already."

"You do?" His eyes were round.

"I know what your father said to you."

"You do?"

"He said to you, Ian, go back to the girl and ask her to marry you."

Ian shook his head, but not to say no.

"It's true. I didn't want to, but..."

Fionna pretended to be offended.

"You didn't want to? Away with you!"

"I mean, I wanted to but I didn't dare. But he made me come. Fionna, I'm such a fool."

Fionna put her hand on his.

"Indeed you are, Ian, a great fool. And therefore I shall say yes."

Ian nearly fell off his stool.

"You'll say yes? But why?"

"Well, they say fools make the best

husbands," she told him. "Now away home and have your father come and see me. Then we two'll get married. After that you and he can build castles, which you do best, and I shall spin and weave and tell you what is good for you, which I do best."

So they were married. Fionna and Ian and his father the Master Builder lived together. In one room they kept the tools for the building trade. In another Fionna kept her wheel and her cooking pots. And in the third they sat and ate and looked out down the road.

One day as they ate their breakfast they saw a knight on horseback rein in his mount at the cottage door.

"Master Builder!" he bellowed.

The builder came out and said, "Here he is. What do you want?"

The horseman looked down his nose.

"The Most High King summons you to build him a castle."

The Master Builder nodded.

"He has sent for the right man."

"It must be the greatest, the finest castle that ever was seen or ever shall be seen."

The Master Builder looked the messenger in the eye.

"Tell your master that my son and I will come soon and the castle shall arise as he requires; the finest that ever was seen or ever shall be seen."

Hearing that, the knight swung his horse round and was gone in a spurt and clatter of stones, leaving the three of them looking after him.

Fionna looked at her father-in-law.

"Was that wise, to promise for what has been and what will be?" she asked.

"Why not?" demanded the mason. "It is known that there is not one who can match the best that we can build, now or in time to come."

"Oh, but there is," responded Fionna.

"Who?" demanded Ian and his father together.

"The two of you," said the girl. "Your best work is still to be. It will end only with your lives. If the King is to have the best work you will ever do, what can that mean?"

"What are you saying, Fionna?" asked her husband.

"Think on it," answered his wife. "Go and build your castle, but be careful how you finish it."

Ian shook his head, but the Master Builder nodded his. "You are a wise girl," he said.

That day, father and son shouldered their packs and took the road to the King's house to begin their work.

They built, and day by day, week by week the castle walls rose more splendid than any ever seen. At night they rested in the King's house and were fed on the best of food. But all the time they were closely guarded. The Master Builder saw the guards and remembered the words of his daughter-in-law.

The work went well but more slowly, and

the King grew impatient as the autumn passed into winter.

At last one day, with the first frosts, the castle appeared to be ready. The masons went to the King.

"Majesty. The castle is ready – almost."

"Almost!" thundered the King. "What does that mean?"

"To complete it we need one tool which we have left at home. We must go back and fetch it."

"That is not needful," answered the King with a dark look. "Tell me what tool it is and I will send for it. You shall not leave the house."

"Very well," answered the Master Builder, "but this is no ordinary tool. You must send your own son. Otherwise, my son's wife will not hand it over."

"Very well," said the King. "My son will go."

"Then tell him to ask her for the tool called Crooked and Straight."

It was agreed. Off rode the Prince, and father and son were locked into their room.

Ian stared at his father.

"What does this all mean, Da? I have never heard of such a tool in all my days."

"Ah, but you have a wise woman for your wife. She knew what the King meant when he wanted a castle finer than any that shall ever be seen."

"What did he mean?"

"That the King will never let us leave here alive. That way he will know we will never build a finer castle."

"What shall we do?" asked Ian.

"Wait and trust your wife." And with that the Master Builder sat down to smoke his pipe.

That afternoon the King's son rode up to the cottage. Fionna guessed who he was and came to the door to greet him.

"Quick, woman," he said. "Give me the tool that is called Crooked and Straight."

Crooked and Straight? Fionna looked at

him with innocent eyes. She knew there was no such tool but she knew what the words meant.

"Come into the workshop, Your Highness. All the tools sit in a great chest, too high and heavy for me to open." She giggled. "I know so little about these things."

The Prince strode past her into the workshop, reached up and swung up the great lid of the chest. It took every ounce of his strength. Then he leaned over to look inside.

"Which one is it, wench?" he demanded.

"That one, Your Highness," cried Fionna, and quick as light she seized his ankles and tipped him over into the chest. Down went the great lid, on went the padlock and before the Prince drew his next breath he was a prisoner.

Next day a message came to the King's house. It bore no name but when the King read it he knew who had sent it and what it meant:

"I have a great bird in my coop. You have two small ones in yours. Fair exchange is no robbery."

Before noon, the Master Builder and his son Ian were set free, paid their wages and sent home. On the road, the King's son passed them riding in the opposite direction. He said not a word and they returned the compliment.

When they were safely home, the Master Builder said, "Fionna, you wise one. How can we repay you?"

Fionna answered with a smile.

"Build us that house only you can build – one finer than the King's."

And that is what they did.

Kari

Kari

· ·

Kari was raking the hay in the big meadow on
Haugen's farm one summer day, and thinking
about the kind of things girls think of at hay-
making time.

All of a sudden she had the feeling she was
being watched. And so she was. For Haugen
himself stood there, stout and whiskery,
waistcoat creased over his broad middle,
round hat over his white curls and long
curved pipe in his gnarled fingers.

"Hey, there, Kari," he said in a very
agreeable manner. That put her on her guard
right away.

"Good day, Farmer Haugen," she said and
went on with her raking. She wished he'd go
away, but he didn't. He stood there watching
her, and smiling.

"Ha hm," said Haugen, clearing his throat.

Kari stopped raking and looked up at him. It didn't seem polite to go on working when he clearly had something to say.

"What do you think, Kari?" he went on. "I've been thinking of getting married again."

So that was the way the wind blew, thought Kari. She had a little giggle to herself, because Haugen was a widower and as old as the hills. But she said demurely, "People do think about things like that."

"Ha hm," went on the farmer. "The point is, I thought about marrying you."

Oh ho, said Kari to herself, as if the old goat hasn't got enough to do without getting married again. But aloud she said, very politely, "Thank you very much, Farmer Haugen, but no thank you."

There was a deep silence. When Kari looked up again she saw his broad back going away up the meadow towards the farmhouse. When he was far away enough, she had a good laugh and went on raking the hay.

But if Kari imagined that was the end of

the matter she was very much mistaken.
Before the month was out, Farmer Haugen
had asked her again, and again. Because he
was a man who wasn't used to being told
no. People usually did what he asked or
told them.

And since Kari had to work for him now
and then to earn money to help her family,
maybe he felt she was obliged to him. But she
kept on turning him down, very courteously
but very firmly. Because if she had thought of
getting married (and she kept that to herself)
she wasn't going to marry him.

Still he didn't give up. The next thing that
happened was that Kari's father, whose
smallholding lay next to Haugen's big farm,
spoke to her, one evening.

"Kari, dear. You're a very lucky girl.
There's any amount of women in this valley
who'd give their eyeteeth to marry Farmer
Haugen."

"Well, let them do it, Dad," responded
Kari, "and good luck to them."

"But he's the richest farmer for miles around. He's got a chest full of silver, and even got money down in the bank in town. He's a real catch."

"I don't care if he's up to his eyebrows in gold," said his daughter. "He's old as the hills, he's as ugly as sin, and I don't want to marry him."

Now her father tried being angry with her.

"You're only a child, girl. You don't know what's good for you."

"I know what's bad for me," returned Kari, very firmly, "and I'm not marrying him."

And he said no more because he knew his daughter well enough not to waste his time.

Kari went on with her work, on Haugen's big farm and her father's small one. The days passed, and she heard no more about marriage.

But Haugen was only waiting his chance. He told his neighbour that it would be worth his while to persuade the girl one way or another.

"You know that piece of land which lies next to your meadow? That's yours the day you get her to say yes."

So Kari's father was determined she should marry the rich neighbour and she was determined she wouldn't. In the end, after several attempts to make her see reason, he thought of a smart idea and he sent word to Haugen.

"Just you go ahead and arrange the wedding feast. Get the priest there and your guests. Then send word you want Kari at your place to do some work.

"When she comes, then marry her, on the spot, before she has time to think. After all, she's very young. She doesn't really know her own mind. We know what's best for her."

Haugen was delighted with the scheme and set about fixing matters with the priest, inviting guests and all. He told his farm people to brew and bake and make ready for the biggest wedding celebration the valley had seen in a lifetime. And so they did.

At last the day came, a bright summer day. The guests arrived and the rich farmer had them all assembled in his best room, ready for the bride to arrive. The priest was there with his book, the kitchen tables were loaded with food and drink. Everything was as it should be.

Now Haugen called one of his boys and said, tapping his nose with his finger, "Now off you get to the neighbour, you know, Kari's father and – listen carefully – ask him for what he promised me."

Then he shook his huge fist and said, "Shift yourself. If you're not back in a jiffy, I'll—" He said no more, but the farm lad took one look at the fist and he was off out of the yard as if his pants were on fire.

Kari's father was waiting for him, and when the boy gave the message he nodded knowingly and said, "You nip down to the meadow and take her with you ... you'll find her down there."

The lad was getting a bit muddled now, but

did as he was told, though he hadn't the faintest notion what he was to take. So he was relieved when he got down to the little meadow and found Kari there.

"Kari," said he.

"Hey there," she answered, giving him a strange look. "What's all the rush about?"

"I've to fetch what your dad promised the master," he said, making sure he got the message right.

Oh ho, who's fooling who? thought Kari. But she told the boy, "Let's see. That must mean the old dun mare, eh?"

He shrugged and supposed it must be.

She grinned.

"Well, she's over the other side of the pea patch, tied up. You take her." And she added, "Don't keep 'em waiting."

So the farm lad ran, untied the old dun mare, sprang on her back and rode like a jockey across the fields to Haugen's big farmhouse.

He found his master waiting impatiently

outside the big room full of chattering guests.

"Where is she?" the farmer demanded. The boy took one look at the fist and decided to say as little as possible.

"Down by the door," he answered.

"Right, now take her to my mother's old room upstairs."

"Hey, how am I going to do that?" blurted the boy.

"Just do as I say," said his master. "And if you can't handle her by yourself, get some of the fellers to help you." He tapped his nose again. "We don't want her doing herself a mischief."

The lad took one look at the farmer's face and decided not to argue. Down he went to the yard and got all the help he could gather. Some men pulled from the front and some shoved from the back and at last they got the mare up the stairs and into the room. There, on the old bed, was all the wedding finery spread out.

Shaking his head, the boy went back to the master.

"Well, it's done, but it was a struggle, I can tell you – the worst job I've had on this farm."

Haugen got his meaning. "All right, lad, your work won't be for nothing, don't worry. Now, get the girls from the kitchen and send them upstairs to help her get ready."

"You what?" the boy was quite bewildered.

"Don't argue," the farmer's face turned red with anger. "Do as I tell you. They've got to get her dressed and down here right away. And tell them not to forget the garlands and the crown."

So the boy didn't argue any more but went to the kitchen and said, "Now then, girls. You've to go up and dress the old dun mare in the wedding things."

They stared at him, so he explained on the spur of the moment.

"It must be some sort of joke he's playing on the guests."

Off went the girls and they dressed the

old mare in all the finery, hanging on her everything they could find. When that was done, the boy went downstairs and told the master with a big wink. "She's ready."

"Very good," said the farmer. "Bring her down and I'll be at the door to welcome her. Hurry up."

The guests crowded into the doorway behind Haugen and waited. Then they heard a scuffling and a scraping, a tumbling and a tramping, a snorting and a clattering. Everyone looked at one another in amazement.

"Here she is," declared Haugen in triumph.

And into the room came the old dun mare, in silken shoes and white gown, wedding garland round her neck and crown stuck over her ears.

For a moment there was dead silence. Haugen's eyes were starting out of his head.

Then someone began to snigger, and some smiled, then others chuckled and others laughed till the whole place was in an uproar.

It all happened some time ago, but they do say that the farmer was so well pleased with his bride, he never popped the question to anyone ever again.

Marusya

Marusya

....

Early one evening Marusya took a pail and went to milk the little brown cow. This was the only cow she and her father had, but she gave such rich milk, that was all they needed.

Marusya opened the battered door, but the tumbledown old shed was empty.

Hardly believing what she saw, Marusya ran to the cottage. Her father sat by the wood stove looking down at his boots. At once Marusya feared the worst.

"Where's the little brown cow, Father?" she asked. "The shed's empty."

At first it seemed the old man hadn't heard, then he looked up, red-faced.

"Our neighbour's taken her."

"What's that?" Now Marusya didn't believe her ears.

"Taken the cow back," her father finished.

"She belonged to him to begin with."

Marusya stared, open-mouthed.

"Father! The cow was given to you in return for all the work you did on his land. Not lent. Given in payment. She's yours."

Marusya's father looked shamefaced.

"He said it wasn't intended we should have the cow – only the milk. And we've had enough milk to pay for the work. He's got a point you know."

Marusya stamped her foot.

"A point? He's got so much money he's rotten with it. He's as mean as sin. Counting pints of milk for days of work! And who fed the cow? What's more, the man's a liar. He gave you that cow. She belongs to you and you must get her back."

Now Marusya's father looked so uneasy that she said, more gently, "Father, don't be afraid of our neighbour. He's just a bully. Go to the Squire. Let him decide."

So, in the end, after a lot of arguing to and fro, that is what Marusya's father did.

The Squire was a big man and rich with it.

He was so well-to-do he could sit on his verandah all day if he liked, in his red and gold waistcoat and his yellow boots, smoking his pipe and nodding to himself. He sat so still, people were sure great thoughts were going through his head.

He agreed to see the two neighbours and he listened to the story of the brown cow. And he looked first at Marusya's father in his threadbare clothes, and his finely dressed neighbour and said, "These things cannot be decided by one word from me. You say he promised one thing. He says he promised another. Who can be right?

"We'll make a test between you. Listen to these three riddles, then go home and come back here tomorrow. The one with the right answers will be the one fit to keep the cow."

When her father came home, Marusya guessed something was wrong – his face looked so miserable.

"What did the Squire say? Do we get our cow back?"

He shook his head. "No, if I want her back I have to answer three riddles and I cannot for the life of me think how."

"Well, tell me what the riddles are," said Marusya.

"First, what is fullest? Second, what is fastest? And third, what is most favoured?" answered her father. Then he went on sadly, "I'm sure our neighbour has the answer. We might as well say goodbye to the little brown cow."

Marusya shook her head.

"Don't give up, Father. Now listen to me. Tomorrow, when you go to the Squire, this is what you must say."

She bent down and whispered in her father's ear.

Next day, as soon as the two neighbours reached the Squire's verandah, the richer one was ready.

"I have the answer, Your Honour."

"Go on then," said the Squire.

"Why, your herd of hogs is the fullest and most fertile, your pack of dogs is the fastest, and – as to what is most favoured – why, that's money. Everyone wants it."

The answer was so smart that the poor man's heart sank into his boots. But to his surprise, the Squire shook his head.

"Wrong, wrong. No good trying to flatter me. I know all you say is true. But it's still not the answer."

Now he pointed his pipe stem at Marusya's father. "Your turn."

So, the old man cleared his throat and began to speak as his daughter had said.

"Earth itself is fullest, for it has all we need to live. Thought is fastest, quicker than anything that moves. And sleep is most favoured, for no one, man or animal, can live without it."

At first the Squire looked amazed. Then he nodded "Good, good. The cow is yours."

He pointed his pipe at the neighbour. "Put

the brown cow back in his shed, this very day."

But he made Marusya's father wait behind and when the other man had left the yard, the Squire wagged his head and grunted.

"Now here's another question and you'd better get the answer right. Who helped you? You could never have thought all that up in a month of Sundays."

The Squire looked so grim, the poor man hesitated. Then he admitted, "I've a daughter, Marusya. She's very bright. I don't know where I'd be without her since her mother died."

"So she's a clever girl, is she?" growled the Squire. And he looked even more displeased. "Well, we shall see just how clever she is."

At these words, Marusya's father began to feel very uneasy. What have I let her in for? he wondered.

"Listen to me," went on the Squire. "Go into my kitchen and ask my cook for a dozen hard-boiled eggs. Take them home with you and tell your *clever* daughter this: tonight she must hatch chickens out of those eggs, rear them, kill three and have them ready-fried for my breakfast tomorrow morning."

"But, Your Honour, that's impossible," the girl's father protested.

"Not for a clever girl it isn't," sneered the Squire. "Now get off, and be sure to come back before breakfast."

Marusya greeted her father with a broad smile.

"What did I tell you. The little brown cow is safely back in the shed and here's a cup of milk to prove it."

Then she stopped at the look on his face.

"Father, why is your chin on your boots? What can be wrong?"

Unhappily he gave her the dozen hard-boiled eggs and told her the test the Squire had set.

"I should never have boasted about how smart you were," he said.

But Marusya just laughed out loud. Then she went to the stove and started to make some millet porridge. When it was well boiled she put it in a bowl.

"Now," she told her father, "go straight back. You'll catch the gentleman at supper. And here's what you tell him…"

Half an hour later, the Squire, mouth full, looked up from his table as a servant showed the poor man in.

"What's all this?" he demanded without as much as a good evening. "I don't want to see you until tomorrow morning."

Timidly the little farmer held out the porridge bowl and said, as he'd been instructed, "Marusya says if Your Honour can kindly sow this millet, mow it, thresh it, grind it and let her have the meal by sunset, she can feed the chicks she's hatched from the boiled eggs and have them ready for breakfast tomorrow."

The Squire brought his great fist down on the table with such a thump, every bowl and mug jumped in the air.

"Very clever, your daughter. Well, she

won that one. That was easy. Now we'll really put her to the test."

So he sent for a stalk of flax which he gave to Marusya's father and said, "Never mind the chickens. By tomorrow she must soak this, dry it, beat it, spin it and weave a hundred metres of cloth."

As the old man left the room, the Squire said to himself, "I'll be surprised if we see that fool here again."

But, to his amazement, an hour later, as the sun went down, while he was having a drink of spirits as his nightcap, there was the poor man at his sitting-room door.

More baffling still, he was holding out a tiny twig from a tree in the orchard.

"What's this?" The Squire's eyes popped with rage.

"My d-daughter," stammered the poor man, "says that you are so clever it will be child's play for you to grow a tree from this shoot, chop it down, saw it into planks and build a loom ready for when she has spun the flax. Then you can have a thousand metres of cloth and welcome."

Controlling his fury with very great difficulty, the Squire said, "Very well. Enough of all this fooling. I want to see this clever girl of yours."

"Of course," said her father, shaking in his shoes.

The Squire went on. "Tell her to come at breakfast. She must come here riding and not riding, shoes on and barefoot, on the road and off it. Then she must bring me a gift and not bring it, all at the same time."

Now Marusya's father was alarmed because he could see that though the Squire was smiling, he was really in a towering rage. When the poor man got back to the cottage he was so anxious he was almost in tears.

But when Marusya heard what the Squire had said, she simply smiled.

"Well, Father, it's late. Time for bed. I shall need to be up early."

At crack of dawn next day, the father

watched in amazement as Marusya bustled about the cottage.

First she threw out millet seed and caught a sparrow. Next she took a young rabbit from its hutch. Then she put on an old shoe, leaving the other foot bare, and finally she harnessed the old billy goat to a sledge.

The Squire's servants stood at his gate, mouths wide open, as they saw her coming up the track.

She came with one foot on the sledge and one on the road. Under one arm she carried a rabbit and the fingers of her other hand were carefully closed.

If the servants were amazed, the Squire was not. Instead he was livid with anger. From the verandah he bellowed, "Set the dogs on her!"

And they did, but just as the dogs, snarling and snapping, reached the sledge, she let go the rabbit. Off it shot down the road towards home and away went the dogs after it.

Marusya carried on up to the Squire's verandah.

"Good morning, Your Honour." She smiled broadly.

He didn't return her greeting, but snapped, "Very smart, riding and not riding, yes. Barefoot and shod, yes. On the road and off it, yes. You've managed all three. But what about the gift you'll give me and not give me?"

Marusya held out her hand.

"Here's my gift – a bird."

Without thinking, the Squire held out his huge hand. But as he did, Marusya opened her fingers and the sparrow shot away, wings beating, off into the open air. He thought his head would burst in his fury.

Marusya smiled again and said, "No matter how clever we are, some things are out of our grasp."

Zaina

Zaina

Zaina was the youngest of three sisters. All were beautiful, but Zaina had a ready wit as well.

They were daughters of a man who stood outside the public baths each day and sold chickpeas coated with sugar. Passers-by would buy some as a treat for their children. But at a ha'penny a packet, the chickpea seller did not earn very much.

In fact he was very poor. He was so poor and humble that, as they say, his nose knew the ground better than the air.

Still, he was proud of his daughters and every penny he could scrape together went towards their upbringing, for he hoped that one day they might live better than he had done. The three daughters loved him for his kindness, and none more so than Zaina.

Every day the three would go to learn how to embroider beautiful patterns upon cloth of velvet and silk. Their teacher lived across the city.

So, every day, when the chickpea seller's daughters walked gracefully along, dark eyes sparkling over the top of their veils, those who had nothing to do – and even those who were busy – would stop and stare at them.

Now the way to their teacher's house took them past the Sultan's palace. And as they walked beneath the balcony, the Sultan's only son could look out and watch them as they went by.

He noticed them, and he wanted them to notice him. But each day, they walked by with their eyes cast down, and never gave him a glance.

He was determined they should notice him. So one morning, he leaned over the balcony and called out impudently, "Good morning, O Gorgeous Ones!"

But the three lovely girls looked straight

ahead and hurried on.

It is hard to be ignored. And even harder if you are the only son of a sultan, especially when you're being ignored by good-looking girls. So the young Prince asked his servants who they were.

Next morning, he tried again. Leaning over the balcony, he said, rather wittily he thought, "Good morning, young pea chicks!"

The two elder girls kept their eyes down and hurried on. But Zaina, who knew cheek when she heard it, gave the Sultan's son a quick glance and answered, "Good morning, old cheese picker!"

Then she hurried on. But once the three girls were round the corner, they all began to giggle. The sound reached the Prince on his balcony and he found it very provoking.

Next day, he tried again, hoping to embarrass them, if he couldn't impress them. As the neatly dressed trio passed his window, he called out, "How's the market in chickpeas today?"

As usual, the two eldest hurried on, but Zaina answered, very clearly, "You should know. Up and down, like the donkey's tail."

Now there was laughter in the street. But who were folk laughing at, the chickpea seller's daughter or the Sultan's son?

This went on for a week or two. Day by day the Prince racked his brains for some witty remark or question that would either impress this poor but not very humble girl, or else put her in her place.

And each day, the crowds would laugh. But if anyone began to look ridiculous, it was not the chickpea seller's daughter.

This could not go on.

One day the chickpea seller was summoned to the palace. A huge armed guard took him from his pitch outside the public baths and marched him, trembling, into the presence of the Sultan's son, where he threw himself down and touched his forehead to the floor.

"Chickpea seller, you have three daughters."

"O Prince of Mercy, that is true."

"You wish them to grow up and marry well?"

"Allah willing, that is my only wish, O Prince."

"Then see that they are taught better manners. No right-thinking man would marry such impertinent creatures. See they behave better, or it will be the worse for them, and for you."

Now the Sultan and his son had power of life and death in the city. The chickpea seller was frightened out of his wits and ran home to tell his daughters.

The two eldest were alarmed, both for their father's sake and for their own. But Zaina laughed.

"Don't worry, O Father," she said. "I'm not afraid of that young ruffian. I know what's bothering him. He wants me to pay him some attention. Well, one of these days he'll get what he's looking for."

"O youngest daughter, stone of my heart's fruit," said the chickpea seller, "I know you are afraid of nothing and no one. But the Sultan's son has power to do you mischief."

Zaina nodded to reassure her father. "It shall be as you wish, O Father. Tomorrow, when we pass the Sultan's palace, my eyes shall look down and my tongue be still."

But to herself, Zaina said, "If that fool thinks he can make me do his bidding by threatening my father, I'll make him think again."

Next morning, as the sisters passed the Prince's balcony, the young man called, "O fairest one, how many peas can a chick eat?"

Zaina did not say a word.

And the Prince did not know what to think. He was peeved when his witty remark got no reply. But on the other hand, he'd shut her up. His trouble was, he wasn't sure what he wanted from Zaina – admiration or fear.

But if he thought that was the end of the matter, he was sadly mistaken.

That afternoon, Zaina went to the street where the craftsmen kept their shops. They all knew and liked her. She spoke to the smith and asked him for a favour. When he heard what she needed, he grinned and said, "O Second Rising of the Sun, to hear is to obey. Tomorrow all shall be ready."

Next day went as before. The three sisters walked demurely past the palace. The Prince was on his most brilliant form. Yet his witticisms went unanswered. He got not a word nor a giggle, not even the twitch of an eyelash. He ground his teeth in frustration.

But that night, when the Sultan and his family were in bed and the servants were clearing away after supper, something strange happened.

In the half dark of the courtyard appeared a terrifying figure, in full armour. In one hand it carried a pitchfork, in the other a razor and a pair of scissors. As it strode under the flickering oil lamps, the metal armour plates gleamed and clashed. And from the sack on the creature's back came a disgusting smell.

"An evil spirit! A ghoul!" cried the servants.

"Run or we are dead!"

They scurried for shelter in cupboards and corners while the armoured figure marched unhindered through the passages until it came to the bedchamber of the Sultan's son.

As it loomed over his bed, filling the room with clatter and stench, he threw himself down in terror.

"Spare me, O Noble One!" he howled.

"Be still, O Miserable Worm!" came a voice from inside the helmet. "Another word and I'll put this fork through you like a kebab."

The Prince lay still. Then to his horror, his nose was seized. His eyebrows, half his moustache and beard and half his hair were shaved and snipped away. He was so distressed he opened his mouth to scream, but the creature stuffed it full of asses' dung from the bag on its back. Then, as noisily and foully as it had come, it went away.

Next morning as the chickpea seller's daughters passed under the balcony, the Prince was there as usual, but his head and face were wrapped up in silk so that only one eye could be seen.

Still, he put a brave face on it, and called out, "Good morning, O silent pea chicks! Aren't we clucking today?"

The two eldest hurried on without a word, but Zaina stopped and looked up at him.

"O Masked One, greetings! How is the beard this morning? Well or half-well? And the eyebrows? And the appetite? How's that after your dung supper?"

And off she ran, giggling.

The Prince thought his head would burst with rage. So it was she who had marched into his bedroom last night and he had grovelled before her. O Humiliation!

Next day he stayed in his room, and the next day and the next, and he brooded and plotted.

Then, when his moustache, eyebrows and the rest had grown again, he sent his guards to bring the chickpea seller to the palace. As the poor man, shaking with fright, crouched before him, he said, "Have no fear, humble but respectable man. I have decided to honour your family. I shall marry your youngest daughter. She is the most impudent, and can be most improved by marriage." He paused for a moment, then added, "If you refuse, the price will be your head, or hers."

The terrified man begged for time to ask Zaina if she would consent. Scared as he was, he would never force his daughter to marry against her will.

To his astonishment – and relief – she smiled and said, "O Father. You shall not die and neither shall I. I am sure indeed that if he does not marry me, the Prince will die of vexation and that would be a terrible thing. Besides, this marriage will bring fortune upon our family."

So the palace made ready for the wedding. But meanwhile Zaina made her own secret preparations. She went to the craftsman's street and spoke to her friend the confectioner. When he heard what she wanted, he saluted and said, "Hearing is obeying, O Daughter of Delectability."

And he made a life-size doll of sugar and icing, as tall as Zaina herself. When the night of nights came, the doll was dressed in her night clothes and placed in the marriage bed.

Then the sisters went, as the custom is, to fetch the bridegroom.

"Yu, yu," they trilled. "Such beauty, O Prince! Such delicacy, such sweetness! Never was there a bride like this! But be gentle or she may melt away at your touch."

They led him to the bedchamber and left him.

When the Prince stood there and saw, in the light of the oil lamps, his bride lying still and passive on the bed, he realized that she was in his power and he remembered all the things he had suffered from this girl – and forgot all his own insults. His wish to have the last word was suddenly so strong it rushed to his head like madness.

Drawing his sword, he struck at the body

on the bed so violently, the lovely head with its painted face flew into pieces.

The sight drove the madness from his mind. Anger gave way to remorse. In his desire to get the better of Zaina, to make her notice him, to admire him, he had done the very thing that made nonsense of all his wishes.

"Fool, villain, murderer!" he swore at himself. Then he took his sword to run it into his own side.

But even as he raised it, someone caught hold of his wrist and held him back. Then the sword was taken from his fingers. He heard a familiar laugh and a familiar voice.

He went down on his knees.

"Forgive me, O Zaina!"

She pulled him up and embraced him.

"The Pea Chick and the Cheese Picker must forgive one another now and then if they are to live together."

And so they did.